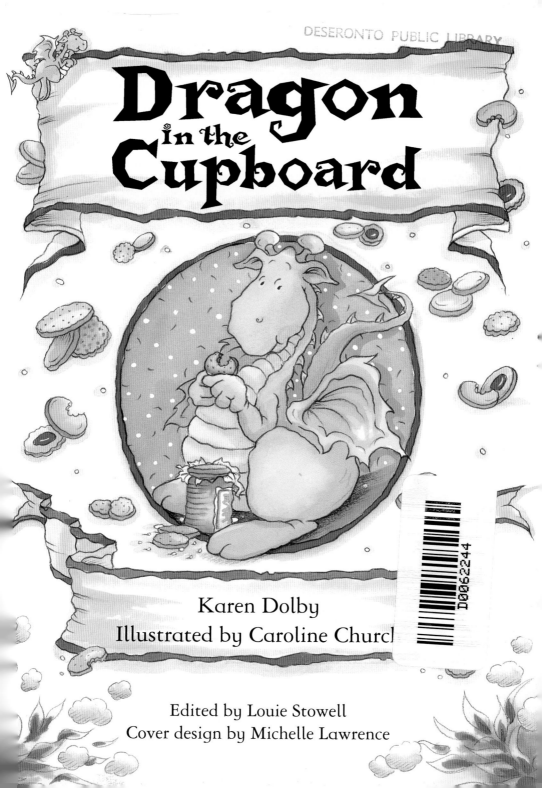

Dragon in the Cupboard

Karen Dolby
Illustrated by Caroline Church

Edited by Louie Stowell
Cover design by Michelle Lawrence

Contents

Snack time

George and Lottie are hunting around for snacks. But what's that strange sound they can hear?

"Is that your tummy gurgling, George?" asks Lottie.

Turn the page for a great adventure.

If you get stuck, there are answers on pages 31 and 32.

Inside the cupboard

The sounds were coming from somewhere in the kitchen. "Crunch... Crackle... Munch..." "That's definitely not my tummy," said George. "There's something in the cupboard!" He opened the door and peered nervously inside.

There, smiling shyly, with its
cheeks crammed with food was . . .

"A dragon!" gasped George.

The dragon looked embarrassed. "I'm sorry, I'm just so hungry," it said, with tears in its little black eyes. "And I'm lost, too."

"You poor thing," said Lottie, patting the dragon's paw. "What happened to you?"

"That's the trouble," it sniffed. "I don't remember. Everything's so jumbled."

Can you untangle the dragon's tale

What's my name?

"The bump on your head made you lose your memory," exclaimed Lottie. "We'll soon get you home now we know what happened."

"But I don't know where I live," said the dragon, bursting into tears.

"I don't even know my own name!" he wailed. Then, he remembered something. "I did have a name badge," he said. "But I lost it. If only I could find it, I'd know my name."

Where's the dragon's badge and what's his name?

Breathing fire

Dan the dragon was very pleased to know his name again. In fact, he was so excited that...WHOOSH! Flames shot out from his mouth.

George and Lottie leaped back as
the kitchen filled with clouds of smoke.
"Whoops," gulped Dan.
George sniffed the air. "What's that
smell?" he wondered out loud, wrinkling
his nose.

Can you see what has happened?

Granny's Secret

George took Dan's scaly paw. "Let's get you out of here before you do any real damage. We'll go to Granny's. She'll know what to do."

"Hello Dan," said Granny. "I knew you three were on your way over to see me."

"How did you know my name?" asked Dan. "And how did you know we were coming?"

"Guess!" Granny chuckled.

What is Granny's secret?

13

The ancient book of maps

"I think I can help you, Dan," said Granny. "Come into my magic workroom." She led them into a cobwebby little den and lifted down an ancient book, blowing away the dust. "This is a map of the Wild Westlands," she said. "Dragonland is somewhere here."

Where is it on the map?

The missing ointment

"Where exactly do you live in Dragonland?" asked Granny.

Dan looked glum. He couldn't think and the bump on his head was throbbing.

Then Lottie had an idea. "Granny, could we put your magic ointment on Dan's bump?"

"Bother, I've lost it," said Granny. "I don't suppose you can spot it? The bottle has a witch's hat on the label."

Where is Granny's magic ointment?

17

Sdrawkcab!

As Granny rubbed the sticky ointment onto Dan's head, he began to remember. "I know, I live in... ELLIVNOGARD!" he cried. Then his smile faded. "No, that's not quite right."

"You're talking sdrawkcab!" smiled George. Dan looked puzzled, then he grinned.

Where does Dan live?

"Now we know where we're going, all I need to do is cast a spell to take us there," said Granny. "Easy peasy!"

She added the magic ingredients to the pot. "Just a pinch of stardust," she said, smiling. "And hey..." BANG!

Cave maze

The smoke cleared.
"Is this Dragonville?"
asked George, hopefully.
"Not exactly," said Granny.   "I, er,
got the spell wrong."

"I'm still only a trainee witch," she said, blushing. "But I can try another spell. Abraca-"

"Let's find a non-magical way out of here," suggested Lottie, quickly.

"Yeah!" agreed George. "I can see a path."

Which path has George spotted?

Granny tries again

By the time they got outside, Dan was starting to wish he'd stayed in the cupboard. At least it was full of yummy food.

He napped in the sunshine on a bed of flowers while the children played hide-and-seek. But Granny was hard at work, fumbling through her spell book.

"Aha!" she cried, waking Dan up with a start. "Here's the right spell! But I'll need a flower with bell-shaped petals and diamond-shaped leaves to make it work."

Can you find the flower that Granny needs?

A fantastic flight

Clutching the flower, Granny cried out
the magic word, "Kazzam!"
    With a burst of stars...

... a unicorn appeared! He seemed to be offering them a ride. Although it was a tight fit, they all squeezed onto his back and he soared into the air. But after the creature left them on a rocky crag, Dan realized something was very wrong...

This was NOT Dragonland. Lottie gulped in horror as she spotted a very fierce-looking beast creeping closer and closer.

What country has the unicorn taken them to by mistake?

Ferocious beasts

There was nowhere to hide. "I don't have time to do a spell," yelped Granny.

"Good!" said George. "They haven't been very helpful so far."

"Don't be mean, George," said Lottie.

Lottie spotted a boat to escape in. But first they had to find a path down the rocky cliff.

Can you see a safe route down the mountain?

Party picnic

Safe at the water's edge, Granny nimbly jumped aboard the boat. But, just then, a wind sprang up. They heard wings beating and a tongue of flame whooshed past, scorching the grass.

With a thud, a small dragon landed in front of them. "We've been looking for you everywhere, Dan," the dragon exclaimed.

"It's Dana, my sister," whooped Dan.

Dan's family and friends were all eating a delicious picnic nearby. "It's easy to spot my family," said Dan. "We all have yellow tummies and green arrow tips on our tails."

Can you spot all the dragons in Dan's family?

Home again

At sunset, Dan's Dad gave the humans a ride home - and Dan tagged along behind. They soared through the clouds and, all too soon, they arrived back at Granny's house. She gave Dan some extra magical ointment, just in case he got confused again.

"I'll visit soon," said Dan. "But next time I'll know the way home, thanks to all of you!"

Answers

Feeling lost or confused like Dan the dragon? Here are the answers to the puzzles.

Pages 6-7

This is the little dragon's story in the right order:

We went for a picnic. It became very windy. I hit a tree . . .
. . . and fell to the ground. I was dizzy and lost. I saw an open door . . .
. . . and found something to eat.

Pages 8-9

The dragon's badge is here. His name is Dan.

Pages 10-11

Dan's fiery breath has toasted the bread, boiled the milk in the mug, and singed the papers and the box of cereal. They are circled below.

Pages 12-13

Granny's secret is that she is a witch. The telltale signs are: the witch's hat, the broomstick and the spellbook, as well as the strange mix of animals in her house.

Pages 14-15

This is Dragonland.

Pages 16-17

Granny's magic ointment is here.

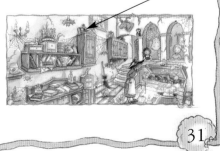

Pages 18-19
The place where Dan lives is called **DRAGONVILLE**.

Pages 20-21
The safe route out of the cave is marked here.

Pages 22-23
Here is the flower that Granny needs.

Pages 24-25
The unicorn has taken them to Dinosaurland by mistake.

Pages 26-27
The safe path down to the boat is marked here.

Pages 28-29
The dragons in Dan's family are circled here.